# Snowboarding

## The World's Most Sizzling Snowboard Spots and Techniques

by Paul Mason

CAPSTONE PRESS
a capstone imprint

Edge Books are published by
Capstone Press, a Capstone imprint,
151 Good Counsel Drive, P.O. Box 669,
Mankato, Minnesota 56002.
www.capstonepub.com

First published 2011
Copyright © 2011 A & C Black
Publishers Limited

Produced for A & C Black by
Monkey Puzzle Media Ltd,
48 York Avenue,
Hove BN3 1PJ, UK

Printed and bound in China by C&C Offset
Printing Co.

032010
005746ACF10

The right of Paul Mason to be identified as
the author of this Work has been asserted by
him in accordance with the Copyright, Designs,
and Patents Act 1988.

Library of Congress Cataloging-in-Publication
Data
Mason, Paul, 1967-
  Snowboarding : the world's most sizzling
  snowboard spots and techniques / by Paul
  Mason.
    p. cm. -- (Passport to world sports)
  Includes bibliographical references and
  index.
  ISBN 978-1-4296-5503-3 (library binding)
  1. Snowboarding--Juvenile literature. 2.
  Snowboarding--Guidebooks--Juvenile
  literature.  I. Title. II. Series.

GV857.S57M355 2011
796.93'9--dc22

2010012527

Editor: Dan Rogers
Design: Mayer Media Ltd
Picture research: Lynda Lines

This book is produced using paper that
is made from wood grown in managed,
sustainable forests. It is natural, renewable,
and recyclable. The logging and manufacturing
processes conform to the environmental
regulations of the country of origin.

Picture acknowledgements
Action Images pp. 5 top (Huber Images/Zuma
Press), 7 bottom (Zuma Press), 8–9 (Gilles
Levant/DPPI), 9 (Pascal Lauener/Reuters); Air
& Style pp. 16, 17; Alamy p. 20 (StockShot);
Corbis pp. 1 (Aaron Black), 10 (Hugh Whitaker/
cultura), 11 (Aaron Black), 27 (Bob Frid/
Icon SMI); Getty Images pp. 6–7 (Donald C.
Landwehrle), 14–15, 19 (Greg Von Doersten),
22, 23, 24–25, 25 top (AFP), 28 (Purestock), 29
(Scott Markewitz); High Mountain Heli-Skiing,
Jackson Hole p. 18–19; iStockphoto pp. 4–5,
21; MPM Images pp. 12 both; Photolibrary
pp. 13 (Bill Stevenson), 15 top (Bill Stevenson);
Rex Features p. 26 (Neale Haynes). Compass
rose artwork on front cover and inside pages
by iStockphoto. Map artwork by MPM Images.

The front cover shows a snowboarder going
downhill (Photolibrary/Monkey Business
Images Ltd).

Every effort has been made to contact copyright
holders of material reproduced in this book.
Any omissions will be rectified in subsequent
printings if notice is given to the publishers.

## SAFETY ADVICE

Don't attempt any of the
activities or techniques
in this book without the
guidance of a qualified
snowboard instructor.

# CONTENTS

# It's a White World

You push yourself to your feet and brush the snow from your clothes. The board starts to slide downhill. You let it pick up speed and then drop into a long, arcing turn. A fan of snow sprays up behind the board in the sunshine. Sound good? Only a snowboarder knows the feeling!

*Dragging a hand as he carves a turn through the powdery snow, this rider is having a GREAT day.*

## SNOWBOARDING WORLD

At any moment in time, there is a snowboarding slope open somewhere in the world. But how can you be sure you'd fit in if you arrived there, ready to ride? You don't want people to think you're a **kook**. So you'll need to know the rules of the game: how to keep yourself and other people safe in the dangerous mountain environment. You need to understand snowboarding's secret language—what's a "heel-edge to toe-edge turn"? And most important of all, you need to know how to snowboard.

## THE SECRET LANGUAGE OF SNOWBOARDING

**kook** clumsy, untidy rider
**piste** marked route for skiers and snowboarders

**4**

*"Let's go that way." "No, over there!" Nothing beats the excitement of hitting the slope with your friends.*

### Passport to Snowboarding

Almost everything you need to know about snowboarding is gathered together in this book. It's your passport to the snowboarding world! Equipment, technique, and other essentials are included. Now imagine you have a dream ticket that takes you anywhere in the world. Where would you go? Turn the page and start exploring.

## Technical: Snowboarding equipment

There are a few basic pieces of snowboarding gear everyone needs: a board, boots, and warm clothes. Most of these can be rented for a first trip. Once they've got the bug, riders often buy their own equipment.

**Clothing essentials:**

• A waterproof jacket, ideally with a snow skirt (an inner layer with a hem that grips the hips tightly, to stop snow from getting inside when you fall over).

• Waterproof pants.

• Fleece, hat, goggles, snowboard gloves, thermal underwear, warm socks.

**Board choices:**

• Freestyle boards are symmetrical (the same shape front and back) and are good for jumps and riding in snow parks.

• Freeride boards have slightly longer noses and are good for **piste** and all-mountain riding.

**Boots and bindings:**

• Most riders use soft boots and strap bindings, which you have to sit down to fasten or unfasten.

• Some riders prefer step-in bindings, which automatically attach the boot to the board (so there's less sitting in the snow!).

# Stowe Mountain

There are lots of resorts in this area of the northeastern United States, so why pick Stowe? Simple: the nearby town of Burlington is home to the company that invented the modern snowboard, Burton. If you had to pick a place where they know their snowboard equipment, this is it! It also helps that Stowe has some great riding for boarders of all abilities.

**STOWE MOUNTAIN**
**Location:** Vermont
**Type of riding:** piste, some powder areas
**Difficulty level:** 1 of 5
**Season:** November to April

## Snowboarding Stowe

This is a friendly resort, and the locals aren't snooty toward outsiders. The riding at Stowe includes Mount Mansfield, the highest peak in Vermont. Mansfield is best for experienced riders. Beginners tend to head for a separate area, Spruce Peak, where the runs are less steep and easier.

*Snowboarding on a beautiful sunny day, on the slopes near Stowe.*

## THE SECRET LANGUAGE OF SNOWBOARDING

**powder** light, fluffy snow

## If you like Stowe Mountain ...

you could also try:
- Jackson Hole, Wyoming
- Chamonix, France
- Zermatt, Switzerland

### EQUIPMENT

**Snowboard:** A freeride board is probably best for Stowe, which has 21.7 miles (35 kilometers) of pistes and fast, modern lifts. Expert boarders will want to try the **powder** at the Tres Amigos and Lookout areas.

**Clothing:** Dress warm for the chilly New England winds! A jacket with a hood to keep out the cold, and plenty of layers, are a good idea.

**Other gear:** Goggles, backpack for keeping spare clothes in.

### Tip from a Local

Take a packed lunch—the mountain restaurants are always jam-packed!

## TECHNIQUE
# Renting gear

There's nothing worse than getting to the top of a mountain and discovering a problem with your rented equipment. These tips will help you make sure you get the right board, boots, and bindings from a rental shop wherever you are:

- Get the right length board. For most beginners, this is a board that comes up to their chin.

- Make sure your boots fit. You need a bit of wiggle room for your toes when your heel is right at the back of the boot. Make sure the boots are well padded and that the tops don't bite into your calves.

- Check that the bindings fit the boots properly and are not too big. Double-check that all the nuts and bolts on the bindings are done up tightly.

*Wearing boots that fit well and are comfortable makes snowboarding a much more enjoyable experience. It's worth spending time in the rental shop to get the right fit.*

# Val d'Isère

If you like company, Val d'Isère is the place for you. This is one of the busiest, loudest, liveliest resorts in the French Alps. From here you can get access to over 186 miles (300 kilometers) of runs, plus a huge variety of **off-piste** skiing. With all those runs, there are plenty of lifts for beginners to practice getting on and off.

**VAL D'ISÈRE**
**Location:** Savoie region, France
**Type of riding:** piste, some powder areas
**Difficulty level:** 1 of 5
**Season:** November to May

## SNOWBOARDING VAL D'ISÈRE

Val d'Isère and the nearby resort of Tignes (a good place to head for if you get tired of the crowds) make up the area called the Espace Killy. Almost half the runs (24 out of 55) are good for beginners. There is also a snow park and a **half pipe** for practicing jumps.

*One of the biggest, busiest resorts in the Alps, Val d'Isère gives access to a huge snowboarding area.*

### Tip from a Local
Don't start your last run of the day too late—the routes back into town get unbelievably crowded.

## Equipment

**Snowboard:** Any kind of board is fine here. With all the lifts (24 of them tricky **drag lifts**) this might be a good place for step-in bindings.

**Clothing:** Like everywhere in the Alps, the weather can change quickly. Check the weather forecast (called *Météo*) at the lift stations, but always take an extra layer of clothes just in case.

**Other gear:** Goggles, and your biggest, coolest sunglasses—the cafés and restaurants are a bit of a fashion parade!

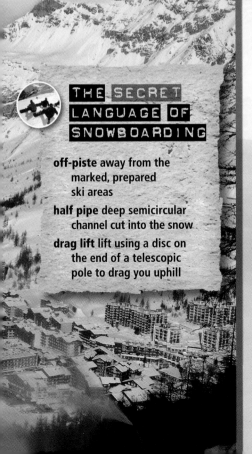

## THE SECRET LANGUAGE OF SNOWBOARDING

**off-piste** away from the marked, prepared ski areas

**half pipe** deep semicircular channel cut into the snow

**drag lift** lift using a disc on the end of a telescopic pole to drag you uphill

# TECHNIQUE
# Catching a lift

The lifts in mountain resorts were designed for skiers, not snowboarders—which can make them a bit of a challenge to use. The most common type of lift is a chair lift. Here's how to get on one:

*Resting your board on the footrest, like the rider on the right, makes riding a chair lift with a snowboard much more comfortable.*

1. In the lift line, take your back foot out of the binding.

2. When the lift gate opens, slide or shuffle forward, by pushing off with your back foot like a skateboarder.

3. Stop on the line. When the lift hits the back of your leg, sit down.

4. Pull the safety bar down (if it doesn't come down automatically) and rest your front leg on the footrest.

# Whistler

Whistler bills itself as the world's best snowboard destination, and there are plenty of boarders who agree. If the winter days just aren't long enough for you, the resort offers nighttime riding, and even summer boarding. There are also three snow parks and three half pipes.

**WHISTLER**
**Location:** British Columbia, Canada
**Type of riding:** piste, powder, snow parks
**Difficulty level:** 2 of 5
**Season:** November to June

### SNOWBOARDING WHISTLER

There really is something for everyone at Whistler. Most of the pistes are best for intermediate riders, but there are still 40 that are great for beginners. As most people learning to snowboard stick to the same three or four pistes, that means there are plenty to choose from. Expert thrill seekers, meanwhile, can drop off cliffs, ride through powder fields, or launch massive **airs** in the snow park.

*Getting a friend to hold on to you for your first run might seem like a good idea—but really it's best to get used to balancing on your own.*

## TECHNIQUE
# Balancing on the board

You've got your board, and you've managed to catch a lift to a nice-looking slope to start on. It's time to take the first steps to becoming an expert snowboarder:

1. Sit in the snow and strap on your board (fasten your leash first, in case the board slides away).

2. Push yourself to your feet, digging your heels into the snow for grip.

3. Once you are used to balancing, put a little extra weight on your front foot.

The board will slide in that direction.

4. To stop, take the extra weight off your front foot. Now put weight on your back foot, and the board will slide in the opposite direction. That's it—you're snowboarding.

At Whistler, beginners can practice their wobbly first moves in areas called Slow Zones. High speeds are not allowed here, which makes it a more relaxing (and safer) place to learn.

## Equipment

**Snowboard:** Bring whatever kind of board is most suitable for the riding you plan to do.

**Clothing:** Lots of the pistes go through trees, so there is usually shelter. Even so, it gets cold, so wrap up well.

**Other gear:** A hooded jacket or balaclava might come in handy for keeping your ears warm on really freezing days.

*Hooo-whee! Extreme riding at Whistler: fortunately, there are also slopes for less-expert riders.*

### THE SECRET LANGUAGE OF SNOWBOARDING

**air** or **"aerial"** this means a jump

# Sierra Nevada

There can't be many places where you can ski with a view of Morocco's Rif Mountains. In fact, there's only ONE place where you can do that: Sierra Nevada in Spain. Closer to the resort are the amazing ancient palaces of the Alhambra, and just a couple of hours away are the sunny beaches of the Mediterranean Sea.

**SIERRA NEVADA**
**Location:** Andalusia, Spain
**Type of riding:** mainly piste, some freestyle
**Difficulty level:** 1.5 of 5
**Season:** December to May

## SNOWBOARDING SIERRA NEVADA

Despite being Europe's sunniest resort, Sierra Nevada has one of the longest ski seasons in Europe. If snow doesn't fall from the sky, they make it using snowmaking machines. The long, wide, rolling pistes are perfect for beginners and improvers to practice their techniques. Only expert snowboarders will struggle to find runs hard enough to challenge them.

### Tip from a Local
On weekends and in high season, don't sleep in! By mid-morning, the lift lines are terrible!

*The main run down into the resort at Sierra Nevada.*

*Sierra Nevada offers deep powder, as well as groomed pistes.*

# Heel-edge to toe-edge turns

*This rider has a nice, relaxed stance as she comes out of a heel-edge to toe-edge turn.*

This is the first turn most snowboarders learn. Most riders sit down to fasten their bindings and then push up on to their heel edge before setting off down the slope.

**1.** Ride along on your heel edge, knees bent and weight on your front foot.

**2.** Let your knees drop forward, directing pressure through your toes and shins. Your hands and shoulders also drop forward and down.

**3.** As the board speeds up through the turn, keep the same body position. If you chicken out, it will race off downhill or **spin out**, and you'll crash.

**4.** Once the board has turned all the way round, on to the toe edge, relax into your original body position.

## EQUIPMENT

**Snowboard:** A freeride board is probably best here, as most of the snowboarding is on-piste.

**Clothing:** High winds are common in winter (and they sometimes close the lifts), so a windproof jacket and pants. Light clothing is OK at the end of the season.

**Other gear:** Don't forget your suntan lotion!

### THE SECRET LANGUAGE OF SNOWBOARDING

**spin out** let the board slip out of control

13

# Thredbo

Say "Australia" and most people think of surfing, not snowboarding. But there IS snowboarding in Australia, and some of the country's best runs are found at Thredbo. The resort has the highest **vertical drop** in Australia, so the pistes are among the longest you can find.

**THREDBO**
**Location:** New South Wales, Australia
**Type of riding:** mainly piste, some off-piste and freestyle
**Difficulty level:** 2 of 5
**Season:** June to October

### SNOWBOARDING THREDBO

At Thredbo, two-thirds of the pistes are ideal for improvers. The resort can suffer from lack of snow, but it has good snowmaking machines and most runs can be ridden right through the season. When it DOES snow, expert riders head for the Central Spur area, where the powder can be great.

*Picking a route through the rocks in one of Thredbo's off-piste areas.*

### Tip from a Local

In summer, the Supertrail (the resort's longest run) turns into the Thredbo Downhill, a killer mountain bike route.

## EQUIPMENT

**Snowboard:** A freeride board is probably best here, but there is a good snow park if you want to practice your freestyle moves.

**Clothing:** It's usually below freezing at the top of the mountain in midwinter, so dress warm.

**Other gear:** Swimming goggles and swimsuit. (Thredbo has an Olympic-sized swimming pool.)

# TECHNIQUE
# Toe-edge to heel-edge turns

Pick a wide, gentle slope for practicing this turn. Until you are used to turning in a direction that's hard to see, it is best not to go too fast.

*Midway through a long, drawn-out turn, on a beautifully groomed piste.*

**1.** Ride along on your toe edge, knees bent and weight on your front foot.

**2.** Shift your weight by lowering your torso and directing pressure through your heels and into the tops of your feet. Lift your hands up and back toward your shoulders.

**3.** As the board speeds up through the turn, keep the same body position. It will help to look sideways, in the direction of the turn.

**4.** Once the board has turned all the way around—on to the heel edge—return to your original body position.

## THE SECRET LANGUAGE OF SNOWBOARDING

**vertical drop** distance from top of highest run to bottom of lowest.

# Air & Style

Each year, the Air & Style draws huge crowds to watch the snowboarding contests and live bands. Past winners include snowboarding legends such as Ingmar Backman, Terje Håkonsen, Jim Rippey, and Shaun White. Today, this is one competition that every top snowboarder dreams of winning—the prize money is over $250,000!

**AIR & STYLE**
**Location:** Innsbrück, Austria
**Type of riding:** big air, quarter pipe
**Difficulty level:** 5 of 5
**Date:** December each year

## CONTEST ORIGINS

Air & Style started in 1993, when two friends decided to organize a contest to see who could do the best single jump. They expected a few hundred people to show up to watch and were amazed when several thousand snowboard fans appeared at the gates. From there, Air & Style became one of the biggest snowboard contests anywhere.

*Olivier Gittler stands ready to launch himself down the scary-looking start ramp at the Innsbrück Air & Style.*

## TRAGEDY IN 1999

Tragedy struck the contest in 1999. When 45,000 spectators all tried to leave at once, six people died in the crush. The next year the contest moved to nearby Seefeld, and in 2005–07 it was held in Munich, Germany. In 2008, Air & Style returned to Innsbrück. (Another Air & Style is also held in Munich.)

## SNOWBOARD EVENTS

Air & Style uses two basic types of contest, **quarter pipe** and **big air**. Both are based around the idea of doing the biggest, trickiest jump possible. A panel of three judges decides the scores. Each rider gets three attempts, and their best score is the one that counts.

Twenty-four of the world's top snowboarders are invited to take part in the contest. There are two 12-rider knock-out rounds, then an eight-rider final.

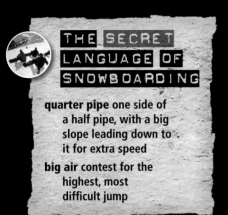

## THE SECRET LANGUAGE OF SNOWBOARDING

**quarter pipe** one side of a half pipe, with a big slope leading down to it for extra speed

**big air** contest for the highest, most difficult jump

*Finland's Eero Ettala midway through a massive, crowd-pleasing air.*

# Jackson Hole

Jackson Hole is one of the world's best resorts for riding steep, powder-snow slopes. It's not really a beginner's resort. Only one of the 56 runs is earmarked for beginners. But if you know the basics and want to improve your off-piste riding, there is probably nowhere better to do it than here.

**JACKSON HOLE**
**Location:** Wyoming
**Type of riding:** most famous for steep runs and access to off-piste
**Difficulty level:** 3 of 5
**Season:** November to April

## SNOWBOARDING JACKSON HOLE

Jackson Hole has the biggest vertical drop in the United States. The highest lift takes you almost 2 miles (over 3 kilometers) above sea level. The resort is good for intermediate boarders, and excellent for experts. Unusual for North America, there are few limits on off-piste snowboarding. The only downside is that when the weather is bad, it's SO bad it becomes impossible to snowboard.

## Tip from a Local

The most famous off-piste run in Jackson Hole is Corbett's **Couloir**. It's for experts only!

*Getting a lift on a helicopter is one way to make sure your tracks are the first ones through Jackson Hole's backcountry snow.*

### EQUIPMENT

**Snowboard:** There are two snow parks and a half pipe, so freestyle boards are OK. But people really come to Jackson for the powder. Bring a freeride board.

**Clothing:** Pack your warmest clothes. Then pack some more warm clothes, hats, scarves, thermals, etc. It gets REALLY cold here.

**Other gear:** A balaclava and heated gloves (did we mention how cold it gets?).

## THE SECRET LANGUAGE OF SNOWBOARDING

**couloir** narrow, steep-sided valley on a mountainside

## TECHNIQUE
# Riding in powder snow

The best place to practice riding powder snow is on a piste just after heavy snowfall.

*Keep the nose up (the board's, not yours!), if you want to pull off turns like this one.*

• For powder conditions, some riders move the bindings on their board back slightly, a little more toward the tail.

• In powder you will need to point more downhill than usual to get the board going.

• Keep your knees bent and your weight centered at first. When making turns, put more weight on your back foot than usual. (If you put weight on your front foot, the nose of the board will bury itself in the snow.)

• To turn, shift your body weight in the usual way. When making tight turns, some riders "bounce." They straighten their legs halfway through the turn, then go back into a bent-knees position.

# Snow Park

At first glance, Snow Park appears a surprising choice as one of the great places to go snowboarding. It has no pistes, and just one lift—compared to the 200 pistes and 33 lifts at Whistler, Snow Park doesn't seem to have much to offer. Don't be fooled, though. This is one of the world's best places for practicing your freestyle skills.

**SNOW PARK**
**Location:** Otago, South Island, New Zealand
**Type of riding:** freestyle
**Difficulty level:** 2.5 of 5
**Season:** June to October

## SNOWBOARDING SNOW PARK

This is freestyle central. Snow Park (no prizes for guessing how they thought of the name) is famous around the world as one of the best snow parks anywhere. It has obstacles and jumps to suit any snowboarder, from someone trying freestyle for the first time to experts practicing their **stalefish grabs**.

## THE SECRET LANGUAGE OF SNOWBOARDING

**stalefish grab** air in which the rider grabs the heel edge of the board behind the back leg, with his or her trailing hand.

**ramp** steep slope

**lip** edge of a half pipe

*Stylish (and very tricky) grabs like this one are a common sight at Snow Park.*

# TECHNIQUE
## Jumps

*Starting small, like this rider, and then building up to bigger jumps is the best way to increase your confidence.*

Jumps are best learned once you're able to ride with the board flat on the snow, without either edge biting in.

1. Head for the **ramp** (pick a small one to start!) at moderate speed. Too fast will be out of control, but too slow will make for a heavy landing.

2. Slide up the ramp with the board flat on the snow. Bend your knees and hips as the board rises up the ramp.

3. As the board leaves the **lip** of the ramp, straighten your legs and hips to help it into the air.

4. As it drops back toward the snow, bend your knees to absorb the landing. Land slightly tail first, and with the board flat (rather than tilted toward either edge). Ride off with a big grin.

### EQUIPMENT
**Snowboard:** Freestyle board, soft boots and strap bindings.

**Clothing:** No need to go overboard on cold-weather gear, and on a hot day it would be possible to wear just a T-shirt and snowboard pants.

**Other gear:** A helmet is definitely required.

### Tip from a Local
Stay late for the floodlit night-riding sessions, and you're likely to spot top pro snowboarders trying out some new moves.

### If you like Snow Park ...
you could also try:
• Whistler, Canada
• Niseko, Japan
The freestyle facilities at both are excellent.

**21**

# Winter X Games

WINTER X GAMES
**Location:** Aspen, Colorado
**Type of riding:** slope style, half pipe
**Difficulty level:** 5 of 5
**Date:** late January or early February

Since 2002, the Winter X Games have been held in Aspen, Colorado. The games are a competition for extreme sports. The summer version features sports such as skateboarding, BMX, and motocross. In winter, snowboarders, skiers, and snowmobilers flock to Aspen for one of the biggest contests of the year.

*Hot action in the half pipe at the 2009 Winter X Games.*

## SNOWBOARD EVENTS

The biggest draw is often the **slope style** contest. Riders take turns to put down the most difficult, most stylish sequence of airs possible. They use a variety of ramps to get the biggest possible height and **hang time** on each jump.

*Shaun White—a.k.a. the Flying Tomato—hits it at the X Games. White is the only person to win at both Summer and Winter X Games. The summer one was for skateboarding.*

The half-pipe contest also draws lots of fans. The finals often take place at night: the floodlights and big crowds make for an unforgettable atmosphere.

**THE SECRET LANGUAGE OF SNOWBOARDING**

**slope style** short freestyle course with a choice of jumps

**hang time** length of time spent in the air during a jump

## THE FLYING TOMATO

The most successful X Games snowboarder of all time is sometimes called The Flying Tomato, because of his bushy red hair. His real name is Shaun White. Around the world,

White is known as one of the greats. He won the pipe contests at the X Games in 2003, 2006, 2008 and 2009, and the slope style in 2003–06 and 2009. He also won half-pipe gold at the 2006 and 2010 Winter Olympics.

# Verbier

Verbier has always been popular with the rich and famous. This is the kind of resort where you could find yourself sharing a lift with a movie star, a famous millionaire, or a member of a European royal family. But Verbier's steep slopes, good snow, and off-piste runs also pull in hardened snowboarders from around the world.

**VERBIER**
**Location:** Valais, Switzerland
**Type of riding:** all kinds
**Difficulty level:** 3 of 5
**Season:** December to April

## SNOWBOARDING VERBIER

Verbier has something for every kind of rider, whether beginner, intermediate, or expert. There are three main areas: Verbier/Mont Fort, Savoleyres, and Bruson. Savoleyres is less steep than the other areas, so it's good for beginners and intermediates. All three have good off-piste runs, and the snowboarding through the trees is among the best in Europe.

## EQUIPMENT

**Snowboard:** Whatever kind of board you want to bring, Verbier has runs that will suit it. For **boardercross**, a freestyle board is best.

**Clothing:** As always in the mountains, it pays to be prepared for cold weather even on a warm day. For boardercross you will need a helmet.

**Other gear:** An **avalanche transceiver** if you go off-piste, and your best designer sunglasses—this is one of Europe's most fashionable resorts.

## THE SECRET LANGUAGE OF SNOWBOARDING

**boardercross** race down an obstacle course of gates, banked turns, and jumps

**avalanche transceiver** electonic device that sends a signal to locate people buried in an avalanche

**hole shot** first place at the first bend

## Tip from a Local

Ask the ski patrollers in the Freeride huts where to find the best snow conditions that day.

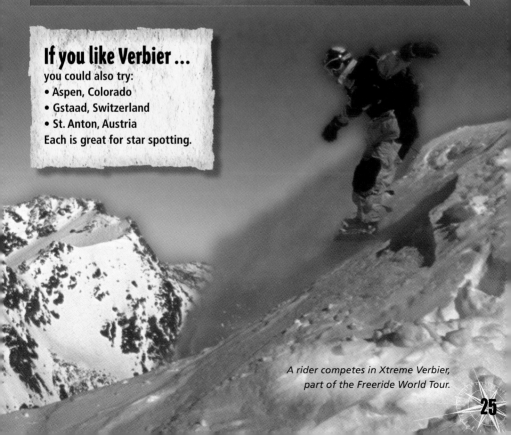

## TECHNIQUE
# The hole shot

Verbier has two boardercross courses, both of which hold exciting races regularly through the season. Like most boardercross areas, they are open to ordinary riders whenever there is no racing going on.

1. At the start, the riders line up side by side.

2. When the start signal goes, they launch themselves down the slope. Getting the **hole shot** makes it much more likely you will win, mainly

*If you like to watch snowboarders crashing, head to a boardercross competition! You won't have to wait long for one to happen.*

because it makes it LESS likely that someone will crash into you.

3. The tight bends and big jumps of the course mean there are plenty of spectacular crashes. Often, the winner crosses the line first simply by not crashing.

# If you like Verbier ...
you could also try:
- Aspen, Colorado
- Gstaad, Switzerland
- St. Anton, Austria

Each is great for star spotting.

*A rider competes in Xtreme Verbier, part of the Freeride World Tour.*

25

# Åre

**ÅRE**
**Location:** Jamtland, Sweden
**Type of riding:** piste runs, some off-piste, but famous for freestyle
**Difficulty level:** 3.5 of 5
**Season:** November to May

Åre (pronounced "oo-ah-ray") offers a different kind of snowboarding experience from almost anywhere else. At the end of the season, it is possible to ride for almost 24 hours, as the sun hardly sets. In midwinter the sun hardly rises, and the resort's floodlights fire up to light the way through the dark for snowboarders.

*Practicing a rail slide at one of Åre's freestyle parks.*

## SNOWBOARDING ÅRE

Only five of Åre's 98 pistes are designed for experts, so the resort's runs are best for beginners and improvers. There are lots of drag lifts, which gets tiresome after a while. BUT expert snowboarders still come here—why? The answer lies in the three snow parks and, especially, Åre's half pipe.

## Tip from a Local
If the slopes are busy, go home, have a nap, and then go riding at night—it's much less crowded.

26

# Riding half pipe

Riding the half pipe well is one of snowboarding's biggest challenges. The steep slopes and high jumps make this a dangerous activity. Snowboarders have developed a few rules to make it as safe as possible:

• Wait your turn at the top of the pipe. Don't try and **drop in** halfway down.

• Only drop in when the rider ahead of you has finished his or her run.

• If you fall, your turn is over. Ride straight out of the pipe. Don't try to climb back up the sides or to gain speed again.

• Keep a friendly face. Cheer others and encourage them, even if they're not very good. Everyone was a beginner once.

## If you like Åre ...

you could also try:
• Méribel, France

## EQUIPMENT

**Snowboard:** A freestyle board and soft boots would be best. There are some good piste runs, but for snowboarders this resort is mainly about the snow parks and half pipe.

**Clothing:** Depends on the time of year. In winter, it can be extremely cold, and you'll need all your warmest gear. At the end of the season, you might see people riding in shorts.

## THE SECRET LANGUAGE OF SNOWBOARDING

**drop in** start riding a slope or ramp

*Warming up for a contest run in the half pipe. The sprayed-on blue lines help the riders spot the lip of the pipe, so they know exactly where they need to land.*

# Chamonix

Say the name *Chamonix* to an expert snowboarder, and his or her eyes will light up. The steepness, challenging slopes, and breathtaking beauty of this valley in the French Alps are famous the world over. Chamonix has been a magnet for mountain-lovers for over 100 years.

**CHAMONIX**
**Location:** Haute Savoie, France
**Type of riding:** good piste runs, but famous for off-piste
**Difficulty level:** 4 of 5
**Season:** December to April

*Chamonix has all kinds of boarding, but it's famous, really, for just one thing: extreme, experts-only riding.*

**If you like Chamonix ...**
go to Chamonix. There really isn't anywhere else like it.

## Snowboarding Chamonix

There are five or six snowboarding areas spread up and down the Chamonix Valley, some of which have to be reached by bus from the town center. Mont Blanc, Europe's highest mountain, towers over everything. Expert boarders come here for the long, steep off-piste riding, but there are also some good piste runs. There is a great snow park in the Grands Montets ski area.

### Equipment

**Snowboard:** Bring a freeride board that you are 100 percent comfortable riding. This is NOT a place to be trying out new gear.

**Clothing:** The best possible clothing for warmth and windproofing. Some of the snowboarding is high up, and it can take a long time to get down if the weather changes.

**Other gear:** Backpack for gear; avalanche transceiver if you plan on going off-piste; emergency blankets for warmth; mobile phone.

### Tip from a Local

If there's fresh powder, get up early and catch the first lift of the day (which you'll be sharing with some of the world's best freeriders).

# SKILLS
# Riding off-piste

Off-piste snowboarding is thrilling, but it is also extremely dangerous. The safest way to go off-piste is with a local guide, who will adapt your route to suit your skill level.

*It might be hard work getting to the top—but it will all become worthwhile on the way down.*

• A full off-piste kit includes: climbing harness, an ice axe, crampons, snowshoes, a transceiver, a snow probe, a shovel, a 130-foot (40-meter) rope, an ice screw, two slings, two ascenders, four screw-gate carabiners—and a BIG backpack for carrying it all.

• You are responsible for your own actions and safety. If you are uncomfortable with anything, retreat.

• Never try anything you feel you cannot safely achieve—it could be fatal.

• Look up, down, and all around: is there anything further up the slope, down the slope, or to the sides that could be dangerous?

• Dangers include layers of snow that could cause an avalanche, hidden cliffs and rocks.

# Glossary

**air** or **"aerial"** this means a jump

**avalanche transceiver** electronic device that sends a signal to locate people buried in an avalanche

**big air** contest for the highest, most difficult jump

**boardercross** race down an obstacle course of gates, banked turns, and jumps

**couloir** narrow, steep-sided valley on a mountainside

**drag lift** lift using a disc on the end of a telescopic pole to drag you uphill

**drop in** start riding a slope or ramp

**half pipe** deep semicircular channel cut into the snow

**hang time** length of time spent in the air during a jump

**hole shot** first place at the first bend

**kook** clumsy, untidy rider

**lip** edge of a half pipe

**off-piste** away from the marked, prepared ski areas

**piste** marked route for skiers and snowboarders

**powder** light, fluffy snow

**quarter pipe** one side of a half pipe, with a big slope leading down to it for extra speed

**ramp** steep slope

**slope style** short freestyle course with a choice of jumps

**spin out** let the board slip out of control

**stalefish grab** air in which the rider grabs the heel edge of the board behind the back leg, with his or her trailing hand

**vertical drop** distance from top of highest run to bottom of lowest

## OTHER WORDS RIDERS USE

**angles** refers to the angles at which a rider's bindings are set. Most riders have their front binding between 10 and 20 degrees forward, and their back binding between 3 degrees forward and 3 degrees backward.

**binding** plate and straps that allow the boots to be attached to the snowboard

**board** snowboard

**boot** snowboard boot

**bubble** small closed lift for 4 to 6 people

**cable car** (also sometimes called a gondola) large, closed-in lift that several people can stand in at once

**chair lift** lift on which between 4 and 10 people can sit

**deck** either the top of the snowboard or, sometimes, the whole board

**edge** metal strip on the bottom edge of the board

**freeride** snowboarding on or off piste, but on natural landscape

**freestyle** snowboarding in a snow park, half pipe or some other artificial landscape

**nose** front quarter of the snowboard

**riding** snowboarding

**tail** back quarter of the snowboard

# Finding out More

## The Internet

FactHound offers a safe, fun way to find Internet sites related to this book. All of the sites on FactHound have been researched by our staff.

Here's all you do:
Visit www.facthound.com
FactHound will fetch the best sites for you!

## Books

*Cool Snowboarders* (X-Moves) by Michael Sandler (Bearport Publishing Company, 2010)

*Snowboard* (Winter Olympic Sports) by Joseph Gustaitis (Crabtree Publishing Company, 2010)

*Jake Burton Carpenter and the Snowboard* (Inventions and Discovery) by Michael O'Hearn (Capstone, 2007)

## Magazine

*Snowboard*
United States-produced magazine carries great features and interviews, along with trick tips and advice from other snowboarders. Has a good website, at **www.snowboard-mag.com**, with a useful buyer's guide section telling you all about the best gear.

# Index